The Adventures of Celtic:

"Tyler and Me"

AuthorHouse™
1663 Liberty Drive
Bloomington, IN 47403
www.authorhouse.com
Phone: 1 (800) 839-8640

Published by AuthorHouse 02/09/2015

ISBN: 978-1-4969-6712-1 (SC)
ISBN: 978-1-4969-6713-8 (e)

Library of Congress Control Number: 2015901656

This book is printed on acid-free paper.

authorHOUSE®

My Boy

The first time I laid eyes on Tyler, I knew our relationship was going to be special.

Tyler is only a little boy, but his love for life sets him apart from the rest of the family. His smile lights up a room. His laugh is so full of joy. His sense of humor makes him seem much older than his 9 years.

I was only 2-months old the first time I met him. But we became best friends from the minute he held me in his arms.

He just stared at me and petted me. I could see a little tear form in the corner of his eye. I was his first dog. I knew I had to make a good first impression.

"I love you, Tyler," I barked in my loudest puppy voice. I don't think he understood me, but he just kept smiling.

"You are so cute," he kept on saying. "I love you so much."

But I noticed he never called me a name. He said words like Ceuta (firecracker), Rocket and Lakers. But he couldn't decide what to call me.

My oldest brother, Zach, finally decided to call me Celtic. But ever since I moved in with my family, Tyler has been "My Boy." Now, it is up to me to keep "My Boy" out of trouble.

Or is that get him into trouble? I can never remember which is which.

Playing Chase

One of my favorite things to do with Tyler is play chase around the house.

I don't know how it starts, really, but he usually screams "Celtic" and comes sprinting at me like a runaway train.

I crouch down, pin my ears back, and start running the other way. Tyler is fast, but I know I am faster. And I am much smaller. I can dart behind the couch, run under kitchen chairs, run around the living room table, and even crawl under the bed.

We play this game until one of us has to stop and rest, or something gets broken, whichever comes first.

"The Mama" always yells at Tyler to slow down. He does, but I don't. When I get on a roll, I don't know where I am going or how fast I am going.

I have run into doors, tables, and all three cats - Rusty, Holly and Patches. They hiss and hide. They are such babies.

But one day, Tyler made a leap for me over the big blue couch in the living room. I jumped on to the table, on to the stand that used to hold our old television, and smack dab into Dad's new 42-inch TV.

I fell straight to the ground. I didn't know where I was or who I was. But, for the first time in my life, my family wasn't worried about me.

They all stared at the TV. It had fallen off the wall and was lying in three separate pieces. Tyler started crying. But he wasn't crying about me, either. He knew we were in trouble.

After I came around, I knew we were in trouble, too. Dad is still making both of us do chores to help pay for a new TV.

But, chores or no chores, when Mom and Dad leave, we still like to play chase. And we also like to wrestle.

Wrestling Around

I think Tyler has been watching too much of those big guys throw each other around inside of a ring that is surrounded by rubber ropes.

I have grown. I now weigh 27 pounds and my veterinarian said I have very strong back legs.

But Tyler is no small boy. He could crush me in a second. I don't think he realizes what 99 pounds feels like when you only weigh 27.

"Hey, Boy," I want to tell him as he flings me up on "The Mama" and Dad's bed and prepares to put me in a head lock. "I might act like a tough dog and all, but please don't sit on me."

Tyler just laughs. He likes to playfully slap me on the face as I try and nip at him. He then gets me and pins me down. But I think his favorite thing to do is roll me on my back and start rubbing my pink tummy.

For some reason, I can't move when one of my family members starts to rub my belly. All four of my legs stick straight up in the air. It is like I am frozen solid.

"OK," I am thinking. "This is not wrestling. But I do love belly rubs. If you want to keep doing that, it is fine by me."

But one day, while Tyler was rubbing my belly, I heard a noise outside. I rolled over and started to bark. I might not be that big, but I am a terrific watch dog.

The trouble is, Tyler didn't let go when I rolled over. He grabbed my stomach as I started to roll. I felt like I was in a bear's claw.

I yelped and twisted the other way. That hurt even worse. By the time I struggled free, I was scratched and bleeding.

I had to spend the afternoon getting bandaged up at the vet's office. I also had to go a whole week without licking my stomach.

"I told you I have sensitive skin," I wanted to tell Tyler.

But I could tell he felt pretty bad. His lower lip was dragging as the doctor brought me out of the office looking like a mummy.

"Here you go, Tyler," the doctor said as he handed me to "My Boy."

Tyler carried me gently to the car and "The Mama" drove us home. She told us we had to be careful and we had to stop wrestling.

"You two have to do something else besides rough house," The Mama said.

"What is rough house?" I asked Tyler.

Tyler just looked at me and winked. He knew what rough house meant. And he was determined to show me as soon as I got my bandages off.

"Just leave everything up to me, C," Tyler said.

Where I have heard that before? Are we getting ready to go fishing?

Going Fishing

There is a real cool pond at the end of our street. It has a fountain in the middle that sprays water in all directions, and plenty of ducks roaming around that like to challenge dogs who are out on a walk.

The pond also is the home of a big, white scary-looking bird. He walks on two legs like a human, but he has a long neck like a giraffe. He also has great eyesight.

The goofy-looking bird will fly up into the trees overlooking the pond and sit and watch. Then, he will swoop down and pluck fish right off the top of the water and eat them.

He is called the "Hunter Bird."

"You know what the Hunter Bird likes to eat?" Dad used to ask Tyler.

"What?" Tyler would ask.

"Nine-year-old boys," Dad would say with a laugh.

I knew that wasn't true. Tyler could whip "Hunter Bird." Even if he couldn't, I would protect him. I don't let anybody pick on Tyler.

"Come on, Tyler," I barked after I got my bandages off from our wrestling match. "Let's go fishing."

Tyler put on my leash and we headed out the front door.

"Celtic," Tyler said. "We are going to give the Hunter Bird a run for his money."

I was so excited I practically dragged Tyler to the pond. But then I looked at him. He didn't have his fishing pole. Harley, who is the best dog fisher on our block, wasn't there. And we didn't have any bait. How were we going to catch fish?

"C," Tyler said, "Jump in the water and scare up the fish. When I see one, I will try and grab it."

Before Tyler said "water," I did my best swan dive in the lake. I doggy-paddled around for a while and then found a school of fish. I dived straight down and made a scary face at the fish.

They started laughing. I came up and barked at Tyler.

"I tried to scare the fish," I said. "They weren't scared."

Tyler laughed.

"I meant get the fish," Tyler said.

I dived down again and forced the fish to come to the top. Tyler was waiting. But so was the "Hunter Bird."

As soon as the fish came to the top, "Hunter Bird" swooped down and snatched three in his claws. When he did, Tyler grabbed the "Hunter Bird" and I grabbed the back of Tyler. We all went crashing into the lake.

"Help," I yelled.

Hunter Bird scrambled to his feet and flew away with no fish.

Tyler grabbed me and we swam to the shore. We were soaked. But Tyler had one fish in each pocket and I had one in my mouth.

"We showed that Hunter Bird a thing or two," I thought to myself.

Tyler just smiled. He knew we would be in trouble from "The Mama." But he also knew this was the best time we had ever had together.

"C," he said, "It is time for you to learn to ride a bike. I am taking you to McDonald's."

Going to Great Burger

When I first came to live with my family, the only place Tyler ever wanted to go was Great Burger.

"What is a Great Burger?" I thought. "I definitely wanted one."

But I am rarely allowed to go with my family in the car. Heck, half the time I have to turn over my water bowl just to get some fresh water.

"Hey, Mama," I scream. "How about putting something cold in this bowl, OK?"

One time, Dad did take me to Drinks & More. That is Dad's favorite hang-out. He loves something called a Route 36. I thought that was a road. But he drinks it.

I like Drinks & More, too. Dad got me apple slices when I went there. They are good. They didn't smell as good as the French Fries, but I knew this was all I was going to get, so I wolfed them down.

But Tyler said Great Burger is better than Drinks & More.

"C," he told me, "We are either going to walk to Great Burger or ride bikes."

I love going on walks, but Tyler hates to walk. He loves

to ride bikes. I can't ride a bike. We had quite a problem on our hand.

"Celtic," Tyler said, "we can put a basket on my bike and you can get in it. I will drive us to Great Burger."

"A basket?" I thought to myself. "Don't we need a ball, too?"

He meant a small crate, but I didn't understand that at the time. I didn't really want to squeeze into a small crate. I hate my crate.

But, a couple days after going fishing, Tyler decided he wanted to take me to Great Burger. He had taped a box to the front of his handle bars. That was my basket.

"I am going to take Celtic for a walk," Tyler yelled at "The Mama."

"OK," The Mama said back. "But only go around the pond. Don't go any further."

I tilted my head. I didn't know where Great Burger was, so I didn't know how far we were going to go. I also didn't know if that basket was going to hold me.

"Are you sure we should do this?" I asked Tyler.

"Come on, C," he said. "We will be home before The Mama even knows we are gone."

I hopped into the basket and away we went. It was so much fun. Tyler made me wear a helmet, but the wind was still blowing my ears straight back on my head.

"Go faster," I barked at Tyler.

He laughed and peddled as hard as he could. Tyler had his helmet on, too. He always wears his helmet.

"Are you having fun, C?" he asked me as we tore through the neighborhood.

I let out one big "Rup."

We made a left turn just short of the other pond in our neighborhood. I knew where we were because we always walked by the other pond. But I still didn't see Great Burger.

"We are almost there," Tyler said. "I can smell the French Fries."

I could smell trouble. But I always smell trouble around Tyler.

We rode a little bit further and I saw these two big yellow arches sticking up in the air. They were weird looking, but Tyler's smile grew as wide as Dad's tummy.

"Here we are, C!" he yelled as he put the brakes on the bike.

I climbed out of the basket and followed Tyler into

Great Burger. We only had one problem. He forgot to put on my leash. As soon as I saw the children's play area, I went crazy.

"Look at that!" I yelled as I ran and jumped head first into about 1,000 red and blue plastic balls. "Wow, this Great Burger is a cool place."

Tyler just let me play. He ordered two boxes of chicken nuggets, large French Fries, and a large chocolate shake. I have to hand it to him. He sure can eat.

"What do you want, C," he yelled to me as I tried to climb out of the maze that surrounded all the plastic balls.

"I want to go home," I barked.

Tyler ordered me an ice cream cone. I had never had an ice cream cone before. It looked like a big white bee hive. But I had to try it.

"Go ahead, C," Tyler said as he held it down for me to eat. "Take some."

I licked it and then licked it again. This was heaven. I couldn't stand it anymore. I opened my mouth wide and took a huge bite of the entire cone.

"Man, this is way better than dog food," I said.

All of the sudden my head started to hurt. It was the worst pain I had ever had. I shook my head, tilted it both ways and started spinning around like a top.

"Brain Freeze!" Tyler said with a laugh.

I didn't think it was ever going to go away. When it finally did, I was too scared to eat anymore human food.

"Want some fries, C?" Tyler asked.

No, I thought. I want to go home and take a nap. The sugar had worn off and I was beat.

Tyler finished his food, put my helmet back on and slung me in the basket. But this time, I fell right through the box.

"Oh, no," Tyler said.

I looked at him and shook my head. I was going to have to run home while he rode his bike. I was in no shape to run.

"C'mon, C," Tyler said. "It will do you some good."

Tyler rode and I chased behind him the entire way. As we turned the corner to Spotted Fawn Ct., "The Mama" was outside waiting. I still had my helmet on. I looked like one of those crash dummies.

"I thought you were just going on a walk around the pond," The Mama asked Tyler.

Tyler knew we were in trouble. But he was a clever little guy.

"We did, Mom," he said. "But Celtic took off running and I had to get my bike and catch him. We found the helmet lying on the road, so I put it on Celtic's head."

"Uh, huh," The Mama said. "We will have to talk to your father about this."

That was not good. I just hope he remembers that he is going to take us to the park in a couple days.

Going to the Park

After Dad gave us a good scolding for going to Great Burger, Tyler and I sat around the house for about three days.

We were bored to death. We couldn't play chase. We couldn't wrestle. We couldn't go fishing. The only thing we could do was play fetch.

Tyler got a tennis ball and threw it around the house. I went and found it and brought it back. I am supposed to drop it and let him do it again. I don't like to drop it. I want to play tug of war.

But after a while, I got tired of that game. We needed a new adventure.

"Anyone want to go to North Shore Park," Dad asked as we were both lounging on the couch.

Tyler is kind of lazy, but I jumped up and ran to Dad faster than our cat Rusty does when he hears the sound of food hitting his bowl.

"Come on, Dad," I barked. "Let's go."

Tyler struggled to his feet and went and put on his swimming trunks.

"You don't need your swimsuit," Dad told Tyler.

"We might need it," Tyler said as he looked at me and giggled. "Celtic might jump in and I will have to rescue him."

Dad shook his head and went and got my leash. After he put it on me, I drug him to the car and then sat in the back with Tyler.

"I love going for rides," I barked.

I knew Tyler had something up his sleeve as he just giggled. Dad looked at both of us with a grin.

"You two just stay out of trouble," he said. "I know that is hard, but it is a big park. You have to stay close to me."

When we got to the park, Tyler grabbed my leash and we jumped out of the car. There were other dogs running around. There were ducks by the big lake. And there were all sorts of things to climb on.

"We are at the zoo!" I thought.

Tyler saw a couple of his friends from school who also had their puppies on a leash. We all were set to explore the park.

"You guys stay where I can see you!" Dad yelled as he sat down by the jungle gym.

"OK, Dad!" Tyler yelled back. "I love you."

Tyler always says I love you when he is about to get

into mischief. But that is why I love him. He is always up to something.

We walked a little ways on the sidewalk and we came to the bridge. It was pretty high, but one of the other dogs, Rex, said he wanted to try and jump off.

"It is not that high," said Rex, who was a black and white boxer with slobber all over his mouth. "I'll bet I could make a big splash."

Rex's boy, Sterling, wanted to jump, too. It was so funny. Sterling was built just like Rex.

"Hey, Rex," Sterling said. "I'll bet we could jump together."

I looked at them and then looked at Tyler. I wasn't going without Tyler. But if Tyler went, I was going to try and make the biggest splash.

"What do you think, C?" Tyler asked.

Just then, Sterling and Rex leaped off the bridge. It seemed like it took forever for them to hit the water. But they made a terrific splash.

"We have to beat that, C," Tyler said.

We climbed up on the rail, counted to three and took off. He held my left paw and I screamed as loud as I could.

When we hit the water, I landed on my back legs. It was great. Tyler went in straight up and down like a pencil. We didn't make the best splash. But we had the best entry.

"Wow," I yelled to Tyler.

But Tyler looked like he was sick. His swimming trunks had fallen off when he hit the water. And Dad had evidently heard us scream when we bailed off the bridge.

"Tyler!!!" Dad yelled. "You get out of that water at once.

You guys are in big trouble."

Tyler swam to the edge of the water, but he wouldn't get out. He didn't have his swimsuit on. I got out and sat right next to Dad. I knew this would be serious.

"Tyler, where are your trunks?" Dad asked.

Tyler just shook his head. They were at the bottom of the lake.

"OK," Dad said. "I will take my shirt off and wrap it around you. Then, we are going straight home. No more park for you guys."

It was a short trip, but it was so fun. I don't know what we can do to top it. But I am sure we will think of something.

Chasing Mr. Fluff

Mom and Dad had just about had enough of our shenanigans after the park. They sat Tyler and I down and explained that we had to start behaving or we would be grounded.

"Is that anything like going to my crate?" I wondered.

Tyler was pretty upset. He doesn't like to be bored. But he also doesn't like to get into trouble. We had to be on our best behavior.

A week or so later, Tyler and I walked over to the football field next to the other pond in our subdivision. There were no football players. But it was a great place to run around.

I was sprinting as fast as I could while Tyler was chasing me. Then, I would turn around and chase Tyler. We both were having so much fun.

"I love you, Tyler," I said as I jumped on his belly when he laid down in the grass.

I started to lick his face when I caught a glimpse of something out of the corner of my eye. It was a cat. It wasn't one of our cats. But it was the biggest cat I had ever seen in my life.

"That thing looks like a giant boulder with fur," I thought to myself.

I let out a little bark, but the cat didn't move. I had to chase it. I took off on a full sprint and the giant fleabag waddled as fast as he could over to the only big tree in the park.

"Ah, ha," I said. "I have you now."

I forgot that cats could climb trees. Mr. Fluff scurried straight up the tree, climbed out on the branch and stuck out his long tongue at me.

"You might have escaped now," I thought. "But I will wait here until you come down."

That was the problem. This cat was perfectly content to sit there on that branch. He just stared at me while his legs dangled over the edge.

"I am not moving, dude," he said.

Tyler started to get worried. He knew the cat would have to come down or his Mom and Dad would come looking for him.

"If that cat doesn't come down, we are going to be in big trouble, C," he said.

"Why?" I barked.

"Because you chased that cat up the tree," he said.

We couldn't afford another run-in with Dad. He threatened to make me sleep out in the dog house that my Grandpa was building for me. I couldn't handle that.

"Hey, fleabag," I barked. "You have to come down. I won't hurt you."

By this time, the cat was too scared to try and climb down the tree. In fact, he was so scared, he started to cry.

"Shhhh!," I said. "Do you want your Mom and Dad to hear us?"

"Yes," Mr. Fluff said. "I want to come down. And I want you to go home."

Tyler and I should have left the old ball of twine up in the tree. But we were too nice. We stayed until the Mom and Dad arrived. We stayed until the fire truck came. And we stayed until Mr. Fluff was finally on the ground.

"Who is responsible for this?" Mr. Fluff's Dad wanted to know.

"We are, sir," Tyler said. "My dog, Celtic, chased the cat up the tree. We are sorry."

I knew we were toast. But to my surprise, Mr. Fluff's Dad just patted us on the head and thanked us for waiting until help arrived.

"You guys go home now," he said. "Your parents are probably worried about you."

He was right. They were. But at least we didn't leave Mr. Fluff up in the tree. I am going to give him a good beating when I see him again.

Catching a Bus

Every day, I sit and whine as I watch Tyler eat his breakfast, gather his back pack and head off to school.

I don't know much about school. But I want to ride the big yellow monster that Tyler gets on every day.

"That is the biggest and scariest thing I have ever seen," I think to myself as I watch him climb aboard. "It is much worse than the Hunter Bird."

But, ever since I had a run-in with the "Quackers" when I was little, Dad doesn't let me get too close to the Big Monster. He is afraid I will upset them and the big yellow thing will hit one of us.

"Celtic," Dad always says, "you stand back here with me. You are not allowed to catch a bus."

"Catch a bus," I thought. "That sounds cool. Tyler and I need to catch a bus. But I don't think Tyler is fast enough."

One day, after Tyler came home and got off the Yellow Monster, I told him I wanted to catch a bus.

"The bus takes me to school," Tyler said. "You can't go to school, C."

I didn't want to go to school. I wanted to catch a bus.

But how were we going to do it? I don't think the bus driver would allow a young Terrier on the bus with a 9-year-old boy.

"You have to sneak me on the bus," I told Tyler.

Tyler thought for a minute and then started to grin. He had a great idea.

"Tomorrow," he said, "I will smuggle you in my back pack. But you can't whine or bark. I will tell Dad you are sleeping upstairs."

I was so excited. I couldn't sleep that night. I was pacing back and forth in front of Tyler's bed. This had to go right. I wanted to board the Big Yellow Monster.

When morning finally came, I was bouncing around like a duck in a rainstorm.

"Come on, Tyler," I said. "Put me in your back pack."

Tyler just giggled. He knew it wasn't time yet. He had to get dressed, eat breakfast and get Dad out of bed.

"Hold on, Celtic," he said.

But as soon as he was done eating and brushed his teeth, it was time for me to curl up in a ball and hop into his back pack.

"Dad!" Tyler yelled, "I am going to the bus by myself today. Celtic is upstairs sleeping."

I made myself as small as I could and I got in. Tyler could barely carry me on his back, but he managed to make it to the bus stop. As soon as the bus arrived, I wanted to bark. But I couldn't.

"Don't say a word, C," Tyler said.

Tyler got on the bus and took a seat near the front. We did it. We caught the bus. Now, I wanted to get out.

"Celtic!" Tyler said. "You have to stay in my back pack the entire day."

"No way, Jose," I said. "It is too cramped in here."

I burst my head through the top of his back pack and looked around. There were kids everywhere. I felt like I was at the candy store.

"Look at the puppy," one of the kids said.

"It is Celtic," said Tyler's friend, Devin.

All the kids came rushing over to pet me. I was trying hard to jump out of the back pack. I wanted to play with all of them.

"WHAT IS GOING ON?" the bus driver yelled.

All the kids ran back to their seats. I turned and looked at the bus driver and smiled. I was hoping I was cute enough for him to let me stay.

"Tyler," said Mr. John. "Is that your dog?"

"Yes, sir," Tyler said.

"You know we don't allow dogs on the bus. I am taking you back home."

Mr. John turned around the monster and headed up Spotted Fawn Ct. Tyler and I got out and he dropped me into the backyard.

Tyler ran back to the bus and Mr. John drove off. I was safe outside, but how was I going to explain to dad how I got outside?

"Rup," I barked. "Rup, Rup."

Dad opened the door and just scratched his head. He knew Tyler and I had been up to no good. But he never did find out that I had caught the bus.

Bringing home Lizards

I love to chase frogs when we are on a walk. But when Tyler and I are out playing around our house or in a field, I have become fascinated by lizards.

At first, I thought lizards might be snakes. They kind of look like snakes, but they have little bitty legs and little tongues.

It is funny to watch them run. It is even funnier when I run after them.

A couple days after catching the bus, Dad made Tyler and I play outside for a little while because he had work to do.

That was fine by me. But it was very hot. We had to find something fun to do or we were going to have to go for another swim in the lake.

About five minutes went by before I saw a lizard sprint across the driveway. I tried to pounce on him, but I have to admit, he had some pretty good moves. He went left and right and ducked under the fence. I was disappointed, but then I decided to look under the fence.

"Tyler, look," I screamed.

Tyler peeked through a hole in the fence and saw a

whole family of lizards getting a sun tan by the neighbor's pool.

"We have got to go over there," Tyler said. "Celtic, I am going to toss you over the fence and then I am going to climb over."

That sounded good to me. I wanted to hang out with the lizards. Heck, I wanted to bring a few of them home.

Tyler tossed me over and then climbed over the fence. We made a lot of racket, but the lizards didn't hear us. They were listening to their iPods.

"We have to be very quiet, C," Tyler said. "These guys will not bite, but they are tough to catch if we scare them."

We crawled along the deck until we were about five feet from them. I then pounced and landed right in the middle of the whole family.

"Hey, dude, get off," the daddy lizard said.

"Yea," said the tiny little son. "Get off. We don't want to have to fight you."

I laughed. These guys were no match for me or "My Boy." But where was Tyler?

I looked around and didn't see Tyler anywhere. Then, I heard him come running back. He found a box we could put the lizards in. He helped me scoop them all up and we took them back into our yard.

"We have to get these guys up into my room," Tyler said. "Then, we can really have fun with them."

I barked at the door and Dad let us in.

"What is in the box?" Dad asked Tyler.

"Oh, nothing," Tyler said. "Celtic and I just want to play hide-and-seek."

Dad was busy, so he didn't pay much attention. Tyler and I then sprinted up to his room and let the little guys free.

That was a big mistake.

"Hey," I yelled. "Where are you guys going?"

But they didn't stop. They ran under the door and sprinted to different hiding places around the house.

"Oh, no," Tyler yelled. "We are never going to find them now."

He was right. We didn't. But "The Mama" sure did. She found one about every other day for the next week. And we always knew when she had found one.

"Ahhhhh!!!," the Mama would scream. "Tyler, did you let another lizard in here?"

I felt bad. Tyler always gets the blame. It was partly my fault. Well, it was mostly my fault. But after all, I am Celtic.

Going to Gabriel's

I had a great time meeting Sterling's dog, Rex, at North Shore Park. He was one funny looking dude. But Tyler said he wanted me to meet another dog.

He belonged to Gabriel. His name was Blue.

"We just have to figure out how to get to Gabriel's house," Tyler said. "I don't think Mom and Dad will drive us over there. They probably won't let you go, C."

I was sad. I wanted to go to Gabriel's. But I know I have trouble behaving myself around strangers.

"I will be good, Tyler," I promised.

"I know, C," Tyler said. "But mom and dad don't believe you. We have to prove to them we can be good."

For the next week, I helped Tyler clean his room. I stayed out of the Kleenex box. I didn't eat the cats' food. And I even was nice to our cats, Rusty, Holly and Patches.

Tyler, meanwhile, did all his homework, took care of his chores without complaining and helped "The Mama" bring in the groceries.

"Tyler and Celtic are being very good," I heard "The Mama" tell Dad. "Maybe they are up to something again."

"No," Dad said. "Not those two. They would never do anything bad."

Dad was kidding, of course. He knew we were always in trouble. But he also had a soft heart. He thought we should be rewarded.

"They have been really good for about a week now," Dad said. "Maybe we should take them to Sonic or something."

Tyler loves Drinks & More as much as Dad. I love the apple slices, too. But we wanted to go to Gabriel's house.

"Dad," Tyler said. "After we go to Drinks & More, could you drop me off at Gabriel's?"

"Sure," Dad said.

But there was one problem. I didn't hear the name Celtic. I wanted to go to Gabriel's house, too.

"Celtic," Tyler said. "I will ask Dad if you can ride with us to Sonic and Gabriel's house. Then, when we get to Gabriel's, you have to burst out of the car."

I didn't know about this plan. But it sounded like it was the only way I was going to get to Gabriel's.

"OK, Tyler," I said. "Let's go for it."

On the way to Gabriel's, I laid down in the back seat and pretended to go to sleep. I thought that was the best way to pull this off.

When we pulled up to the house, Tyler opened the back door and I sprinted out.

"Blue!!!!," I yelled. "I am here. Let's play!"

Gabriel and Blue came outside when they heard me bark. Blue was a Bulldog. He looked like a brown and black tank that had been chasing parked cars all of his life.

"Hey, Gabriel," Tyler said.

"Hey, Tyler," Gabriel answered back. "I didn't know you were going to bring Celtic. This is going to be so much fun."

Dad wanted me to get back in the car. But Gabriel's Mom came outside and said it was OK if I stayed. Our plan had worked.

"Are you sure?" Dad said. "Celtic can be a pretty wild guy."

"Sure," Gabriel's Mom said. "They just have to stay outside."

Outside? I wanted to play with Blue, but I don't like to stay outside very long. I have very sensitive skin.

"Tyler," I barked. "You go ahead on this one. It is too hot for me. I forgot to put on my sun tan lotion."

Tyler was upset, but he knew I was not an outside dog. He went inside with Gabriel and I got back in the car with Dad.

"Good boy, Celtic," Dad said.

That was the first time I had heard that in a long time. I smiled and went to sleep.

Going to the Dog Pound

Tyler and I were outside playing in the front yard a couple days later when we saw the Dog Catcher snatch two stray dogs down by the pond.

It was very sad. I knew the dogs were going to be separated from their families at the Dog Pound.

"Hey, C," Tyler said. "We have to find out where the Dog Pound is so we can go let those guys out. That is not fair to their families."

I agreed.

But I knew letting the dogs out of the Dog Pound would be the most dangerous thing Tyler and I had ever done.

"I will ask The Mama," Tyler said. "She will just think I am curious. I am always asking questions about everything."

Sure enough, Tyler asked "The Mama." And "The Mama" told him the Dog Pound was right by the fireworks stand where I first met my family.

"I know where that is, C," Tyler said. "We can get there. We can do this."

Tyler called Grandpa later that day and said he wanted to go to Pizza Plus on Thursday night. Grandpa always takes Tyler to Pizza Plus.

"OK, Tyler-man," Grandpa said. "I will pick you up at 7 p.m."

At 6 p.m. Thursday, Tyler told me to act like I was sick. I started coughing and sneezing. I even sat under the heat lamp to make it seem like I had a temperature.

"Mom," Tyler said. "I think Celtic is sick. He feels warm."

"The Mama" felt my head and she agreed.

"Maybe he can just go with Grandpa and me to Pizza Plus," Tyler said. "We can drop him off at the vet next to the Dog Pound and they can have a look at him. It is very close to Pizza Plus."

"The Mama" thought that was a good idea. Tyler called Grandpa and told him the plan.

"OK, Tyler," he said. "Just be ready."

We waited outside for Grandpa and then climbed in the back of the car after he arrived.

"Celtic," Tyler said. "When we get to the vet, I will take you in. You have to act sick again. Once they admit you, then you can sneak over to the Dog Pound and let the other dogs out."

We drove up to the vet's office and I started coughing

and wheezing again. Tyler took me inside and I let out a couple sneezes. The vet on duty said he would look at me inside.

"OK, Celtic," Tyler said. "Do your stuff."

Once I got inside, I slipped away from the veterinarian, ran over to the Dog Pound, started unlocking as many cages as I could and then sprinted out the back door.

I turned around and saw almost 100 dogs following me. It was the greatest thing I had ever seen.

But there was one problem. How was I going to get home? Tyler and I hadn't talked about when or where they were going to pick me up. And I couldn't stay at the Dog Pound.

I was on a road trip again. Only this time, I was all by myself.

Printed in the United States
By Bookmasters